Dear Parent:
Your child's love of reading starts here!

Every child learns to read in a different way and at his or her own speed. Some go back and forth between reading levels and read favorite books again and again. Others read through each level in order. You can help your young reader improve and become more confident by encouraging his or her own interests and abilities. From books your child reads with you to the first books he or she reads alone, there are I Can Read Books for every stage of reading:

SHARED READING
Basic language, word repetition, and whimsical illustrations, ideal for sharing with your emergent reader

BEGINNING READING
Short sentences, familiar words, and simple concepts for children eager to read on their own

READING WITH HELP
Engaging stories, longer sentences, and language play for developing readers

READING ALONE
Complex plots, challenging vocabulary, and high-interest topics for the independent reader

ADVANCED READING
Short paragraphs, chapters, and exciting themes for the perfect bridge to chapter books

I Can Read Books have introduced children to the joy of reading since 1957. Featuring award-winning authors and illustrators and a fabulous cast of beloved characters, I Can Read Books set the standard for beginning readers.

A lifetime of discovery begins with the magical words **"I Can Read!"**

*Visit www.icanread.com for information
on enriching your child's reading experience.*

JJ
Parish

For my father, the doctor
—H.P.

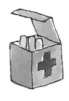

For Michael and Bryce
—L.S.

Aug, 2003

Watercolors and a black pen were used for the full-color art.

HarperCollins®, ♣®, and I Can Read Book® are trademarks of HarperCollins Publishers.

Library of Congress Cataloging-in-Publication Data

Parish, Herman.
  Calling doctor Amelia Bedelia / Herman Parish ; pictures by Lynn Sweat.
    p. cm. — (An I can read book)
  "Greenwillow Books"
  Summary: When the literal-minded Amelia Bedelia helps out at her doctor's office one busy day, nothing seems to go quite right until Amelia begins to treat the impatient patients.
    ISBN-10: 0-06-001421-0 (trade bdg.) — ISBN-13: 978-0-06-001421-6 (trade bdg.)
    ISBN-10: 0-06-001422-9 (lib. bdg.) — ISBN-13: 978-0-06-001422-3 (lib. bdg.)
    ISBN-10: 0-06-008780-3 (pbk.) — ISBN-13: 978-0-06-008780-7 (pbk.)
    [1. Medical care—Fiction. 2. Household employees—Fiction. 3. Humorous stories.] I. Sweat, Lynn, ill. II. Title.
PZ7.P2185 Cal 2002   2002017510
[Fic]—dc21   CIP
                                                                    AC

15 SCP 30 29 28 27 26 25 24 23 22 21
❖
Originally published by Greenwillow Books, an imprint of HarperCollins Publishers, in 2002.

I Can Read!

READING
2
WITH HELP

Calling Doctor Amelia Bedelia

by Herman Parish
pictures by Lynn Sweat

HarperCollins*Publishers*

It was a hot day in August.

Mr. Rogers was even hotter.

"Amelia Bedelia," yelled Mr. Rogers,

"what are you doing?"

"What's wrong?" said Amelia Bedelia.

"You said it was hot enough to . . ."

"Stop!" said Mr. Rogers.

"I said it was hot enough to fry an egg

on the sidewalk. Not on my car."

"Well," said Amelia Bedelia,

"you should be glad.

I would never fry your eggs

on a dirty old sidewalk."

"Forget about eggs,"

said Mr. Rogers.

"You will be late

for your appointment

with Dr. Horton.

Jump in the car."

"Yes, sir," said Amelia Bedelia.

She bounced up and down
on her seat.

"Sit still," said Mr. Rogers.

"Good," said Amelia Bedelia.

"It wasn't easy

to jump in your car."

Mr. Rogers shook his head.

"What kind of doctor is Dr. Horton?"

he asked.

"The best kind," said Amelia Bedelia.

"She is a very good doctor."

"Of course," said Mr. Rogers.

"I mean, who does Dr. Horton treat?"

"Everyone," said Amelia Bedelia.

"And she treats good boys and girls

to ice cream."

They arrived at Dr. Horton's office.

Mr. Rogers took out a bottle.

"What are those pills?"

asked Amelia Bedelia.

"They are for a headache,"

said Mr. Rogers.

"Why do you want a headache?"

asked Amelia Bedelia.

"I have a headache now,"

said Mr. Rogers.

"Then why do you want

another one?"

asked Amelia Bedelia.

"I don't," said Mr. Rogers.

"In fact, I am getting rid

of my biggest headache.

Good-bye!"

"Good-bye!"

said Amelia Bedelia.

"Thanks for the ride.

And I hope you feel better."

"Thank you," said Mr. Rogers.

"Call me when you are done."

Amelia Bedelia opened the door

to Dr. Horton's office.

It was a lot noisier than usual.

"Amelia Bedelia!" said Nurse Ames.

"You are a sight for sore eyes."

"How terrible," said Amelia Bedelia.

"I am sorry that your eyes hurt."

"My eyes are fine," said Nurse Ames.

"But I am up to my eyeballs

in patients.

Dr. Horton had to visit the hospital.

Would you give me a hand

until she gets back?"

"No," said Amelia Bedelia.

"Both my hands are attached to me.

But I would be glad to help you."

Right then the telephone rang.

"Hello, this is Dr. Horton's office,"

said Amelia Bedelia.

"This is Mrs. Bender," said a woman.

"I am calling because I've got hives."

"That's great!" said Amelia Bedelia.

"I'll bet you have honey."

17

"Don't call me 'honey,'"

said Mrs. Bender.

"Do you know what it means

to have hives?"

"I sure do—honey!"

said Amelia Bedelia.

18

"Stop calling me 'honey'!"

said Mrs. Bender.

"I am coming down

to see Dr. Horton right now."

"Good," said Amelia Bedelia.

"Please bring us some honey."

Mrs. Bender hung up on her.

"Guess what?" said Amelia Bedelia.

"Mrs. Bender is coming to see us."

"Oh, my," said Nurse Ames.

"Mrs. Bender is a pain in the neck.

But her heart is in the right place."

"Wow!" said Amelia Bedelia.

"It would be terrible

if her heart were down in her foot."

20

"This is April," said Nurse Ames.

"She is a little scared.

Will you take her temperature?"

"I will try," said Amelia Bedelia.

"Give it a shot," said Nurse Ames.

"A shot!" wailed April.

"Don't worry," said Nurse Ames.

"It is just a thermometer.

Amelia Bedelia, will you tell me

the temperature in three minutes?"

"I don't have a watch,"
said Amelia Bedelia.
"Look out the window,"
said Nurse Ames.
"The bank across the street
has a big clock."

Brrrrrr-ING!

Amelia Bedelia was busier than ever.

She answered call after call

after call.

"I've caught some kind of bug."

"I hope you let it go. Bugs can bite."

"Oh, Amelia Bedelia,"

said Nurse Ames.

"Don't forget about the temperature."

Amelia Bedelia ran to the window.

"It says ninety-eight degrees."

"Fine," said Nurse Ames.

"Ninety-eight is normal."

"Yes," said Amelia Bedelia,

"that is normal for August."

"For August?" said Nurse Ames.

"Don't you mean for April?"

Finally, April smiled.

A boy came into the office.

"Excuse me," he said.

"I am here for a test."

"Then you must be lost,"

said Amelia Bedelia.

"You have to go to school

to take a test."

29

"I am here for a blood test,"

said the boy.

"Blood test?" asked Amelia Bedelia.

"What kind of crazy test is that?

True or false?"

"I wish it were," said the boy.

"Well," said Amelia Bedelia,

"let's give it a try.

True or false: Do you have blood?"

"True," he said.

"Of course I have blood."

"Then you pass,"

said Amelia Bedelia.

"What if I didn't have blood?"

asked the boy.

"Then you would pass out,"

said Amelia Bedelia.

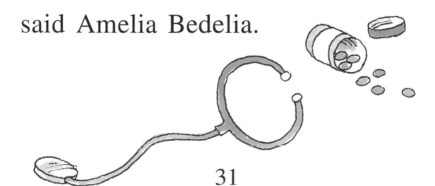

31

"Hi, Andy," said Nurse Ames.
"We need to draw your blood.
Amelia Bedelia, please take Andy
to the examination room."

"Look at all this blank paper,"

said Amelia Bedelia.

"Andy, why don't you draw

your own blood?"

Amelia Bedelia gave Andy

a big red pen.

He began to draw.

34

"My mom told me," said Andy,

"that when you draw blood,

I will feel a little stick."

Amelia Bedelia looked all around.

"Here," she said.

"Feel this old ice cream stick."

"Those depress your tongue,"
said Andy.

"Right you are," said Amelia Bedelia.

"A stick without ice cream
would depress anyone's tongue."

"That reminds me,"

said Amelia Bedelia.

She made a phone call.

As soon as she hung up,

the phone rang again.

"Dr. Horton's office,"

said Amelia Bedelia.

"I have a problem," said a man.

"I am a little hoarse."

"A little horse? Hah!"

said Amelia Bedelia.

"You can't fool me.

A pony can't talk."

"I have a frog in my throat,"

the man croaked.

"Yuck!" said Amelia Bedelia.

"Spit it out!"

"Listen to me," he said.

"I'm as sick as a dog."

"Make up your mind,"

said Amelia Bedelia.

"Pony, frog, or dog?

Maybe you should call a vet."

"I am coming down there,"

he said, and hung up.

The phone rang again.

"Dr. Horton's office,"

said Amelia Bedelia.

"Hello, my office," joked Dr. Horton.

"Hi, Dr. Horton,"

said Amelia Bedelia.

"I have been helping Nurse Ames."

"How nice of you," said Dr. Horton.

"So much has happened,"

said Amelia Bedelia.

"But best of all,

April is normal for August."

"April? August? What?"

said Dr. Horton.

"Then I gave Andy a blood test,"

said Amelia Bedelia.

"You drew Andy's blood?"

asked Dr. Horton.

"No," said Amelia Bedelia.

"Andy drew his own blood.

The table is covered with it."

"What?" shouted Dr. Horton.

"Are you treating my patients?"

"Not yet," said Amelia Bedelia,

"but I will soon."

"Don't tease me," said Dr. Horton.

"I am almost out of patience."

"Oh, no, you're not,"

said Amelia Bedelia.

"Your office is full of patients!"

"I will be right there,"

said Dr. Horton.

The office door burst open.

"Out of my way!" yelled a woman.

"I am Mrs. Bender.

Just look at my hives!"

"How nice!" said Amelia Bedelia.

"You came to bring us honey!

But first let's take care

of that pain in your neck."

Amelia Bedelia began to wrap

Mrs. Bender in bandages.

But she did not finish the job.

All the patients Amelia Bedelia

had upset on the phone

stormed into the waiting room.

Just then Dr. Horton walked in.

"Calm down," said Dr. Horton.

"I will take care of everyone."

50

MY THROAT!
OH, MY STOMACH!
MY HEAD ACHES!
MY NOSE HURTS!
STOP THAT RINGING!

Dr. Horton looked

at the crowd in her office.

"Who is first?" she asked.

"Me!" said the delivery man.

"This ice cream is starting to melt."

"What ice cream?" said Dr. Horton.

"Your ice cream," said Amelia Bedelia.

"I told you I was treating

your patients."

Dr. Horton laughed.

"Good for you," she said.

"My patient patients

all deserve a treat."

They were enjoying their ice cream

when Mr. Rogers arrived.

"Amelia Bedelia!" said Mr. Rogers.

"I was worried. Why didn't you call?"

"I have been busy,"

said Amelia Bedelia.

"Yes," said Dr. Horton.

"She was a huge help.

And you must be Mr. Rogers."

"Pleased to meet you,"

said Mr. Rogers.

Dr. Horton looked at Mr. Rogers.

"Do you feel okay?" asked Dr. Horton.

"You don't look very good."

"We know that," said Amelia Bedelia.

"But we have gotten used to him."

"Say 'ahhh,'" said Dr. Horton.

"Uh-oh," said Mr. Rogers.

"Not 'uh-oh,'" said Amelia Bedelia.

"Say 'ahhhhhh!' Like this."

"Ah-hah!" said Dr. Horton.
"I knew it. Amelia Bedelia,
take Mr. Rogers home
and get him into bed."

"I am as strong as an ox!"

said Mr. Rogers.

"Yes, dear," said Mrs. Rogers.

"And as stubborn as a mule . . .

with chicken pox."

"Speaking of chickens,"

said Amelia Bedelia,

"here is some homemade chicken soup."

"Yum!" said Mr. Rogers.

"This hits the spot."

"Which spot?" asked Amelia Bedelia.

"That big spot on your cheek,

or that little spot on your chin,

or maybe the teeny-tiny spot on . . . ?"

"Enough," said Mr. Rogers.

"Okay," said Amelia Bedelia.

"I will go and wash those eggs

off your car."

"Good idea," said Mr. Rogers.

"Put some wax on it, too."

"Sure thing," said Amelia Bedelia.

Amelia Bedelia got a pail

and some water.

And she did not forget the wax.